The Snapdragon Princess

by
Kim Parrish
&
Deb Landry

Illustrations by
Christina St. Cyr

ISBN 9780977373864

Library of Congress Control Number
2008944312

Printed in the USA
Published by Bryson Taylor Publishing
199 New County Road
Saco, Maine 04072
www.brysontaylorpublishing.com
Edited by Patricia Evans
Cover design Donna Berger
©Copyright 2009 BTP

First Print: June 2009

Dedications

This book is dedicated to my mother Kathryn, who raised me to be a strong, independent woman, able to face any challenge with grace and strength, and to my son, Chase, who helps me relive my childhood every day.

Kim Parrish

In memory of my grandmother, Delia Lynch Bryson, who gave me the priceless gift of unconditional love. And dedicated to my grandchildren, Samantha, Gabriel and Abbey, for memories past and yet to come.

Deb Landry

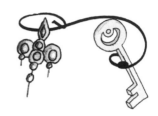

Foreword

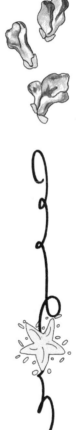
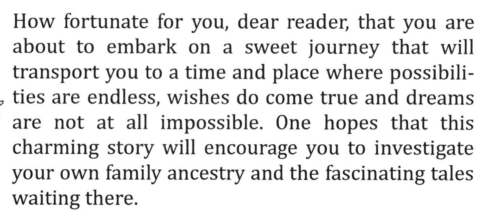

How fortunate for you, dear reader, that you are about to embark on a sweet journey that will transport you to a time and place where possibilities are endless, wishes do come true and dreams are not at all impossible. One hopes that this charming story will encourage you to investigate your own family ancestry and the fascinating tales waiting there.

Most Sincerely,

Lee Meriwether
Miss America, 1955

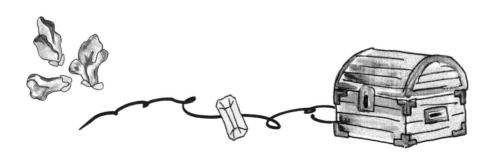

Skipping up the front walk of her grandmother's house, McKenzie was excited for the milk and cookies she knew Grandma would have waiting for her.

The sidewalk was lined with vibrant flowers in a rainbow of colors and sweet, refreshing scents. Grandma sat on the front porch in an old wooden swing. She rocked back and forth, enjoying the warm weather and the cool breeze.

McKenzie dashed up the path to the wrap-around porch where her grandmother waited with a huge hug and a plate of homemade molasses cookies.

"How was school today, Kenzie?" Grandma asked.

"Great!" said McKenzie dashing down the walkway, hopping, twirling, and gathering a handful of snapdragon flowers.

"When I grow up I want to be a princess," said McKenzie, turning around and walking elegantly towards her grandmother while pretending to wave to a group of her adoring fans.

"Kenzie, you are *already* a princess! You're my Snapdragon Princess." They laughed.

Her grandmother pointed to an old trunk she had found in the attic and had brought downstairs for McKenzie to explore.

"Didn't you notice my treasure chest of memories, Kenzie?" asked Grandma.

"What's in it?" questioned McKenzie as she approached with curiosity and caution.

"Let's find out! Here's the key that will unlock the stories of my life and your imagination," said Grandma.

McKenzie gently grabbed the rusty old key from her grandmother's hand and ran to unlock the weathered chest. She wondered what kinds of memories such an old, musty trunk would reveal.

"Grandma, what is this?" McKenzie eagerly asked her grandmother in amazement.

The hinges creaked as she lifted the top, peeking inside with amazement. Its magical contents lured her with their possibilities. She found diplomas and graduation caps, a factory uniform and name-tag, and diaries filled with stories of days long ago. Something incredibly special and somewhat out of place caught her eye. She spotted a gleaming crown of rhinestones and a stunning rose gown amid all the drab, old items. "Were you a princess? Why didn't you tell me?" asked McKenzie.

Her grandmother smiled and, as if it were just yesterday, began to tell stories of when she wore the sparkling crown and flowing gown so many years ago.

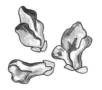

The next day at school, McKenzie was still feeling inspired by her grandmother's story.

"Time for class," exclaimed the teacher as everyone scurried to their seats.

Mr. Young went on to explain that the school would be celebrating American History Week soon, and would hold a big assembly featuring students from each class. Each grade would report on a different era. He asked for volunteers from his class to report on leaders or extraordinary people from the 1940's who were inspiring and had accomplished great things.

"I'll post a sign-up sheet on the board. If you want to participate in the assembly, please write your name and the name of the person from the 1940's you plan to report on," said Mr. Young.

After class, a handful of kids gathered around the teacher's desk. Most of the girls didn't seem interested in participating as many had trouble naming a person from that period in history that inspired them, especially a woman. They whispered to each other that history books were filled with great leaders, but most of those leaders were men.

That didn't stop McKenzie. She knew exactly who she wanted to write about and just the person to help her with the project. She wrote the name on the sign-up sheet and then scribbled her name in as the Snapdragon Princess.

Billy was the next in line. He chose Jackie Robinson, the first African-American to play professional baseball. One day he hoped to follow in his footsteps.

Clay was next. He signed up to report on FDR, Franklin Delano Roosevelt, the 32nd President of the United States. Clay was in a wheelchair and he was inspired that a man led our country from a wheelchair and received great respect from world leaders and the American people.

Brian, another student, also decided to speak about a president, Dwight D. Eisenhower, the 34th President of the United States and a five star general in the United States Army. Brian also hoped to serve his country when he grew up.

Every afternoon for the next two weeks, McKenzie rushed home to work on her project with her grandmother.

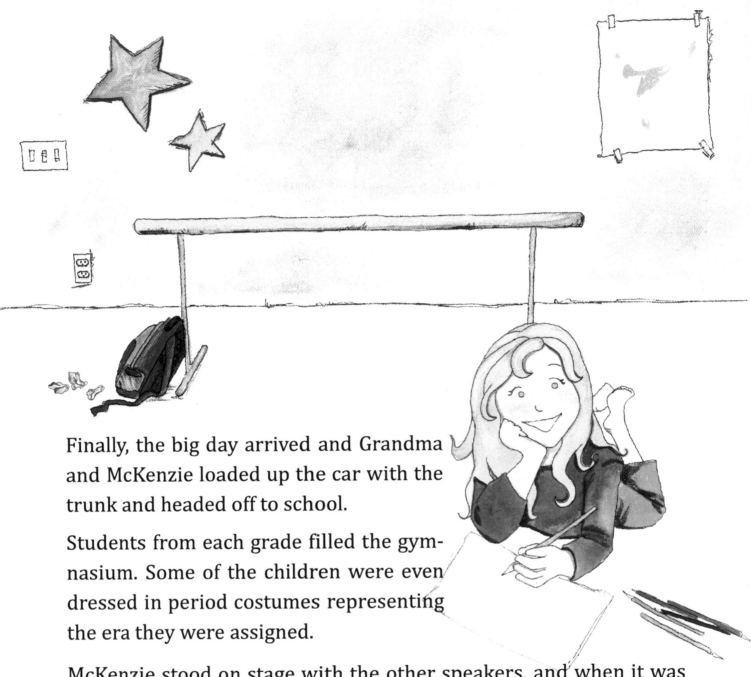

Finally, the big day arrived and Grandma and McKenzie loaded up the car with the trunk and headed off to school.

Students from each grade filled the gymnasium. Some of the children were even dressed in period costumes representing the era they were assigned.

McKenzie stood on stage with the other speakers, and when it was her turn, wheeled the antique trunk to the middle of the stage. Dressed in Grandmother's rose gown and balancing the crown on her head, she began telling the story of a little girl who grew up in a small factory town in the 1940's and dreamed of one day being a princess. She described how times were hard during the war and children didn't have as many luxuries as they do today. Sometimes this little girl would go without toys, new clothes or even shoes because her family couldn't afford them, but she also never lost sight of her ambition to attend college.

One day, both came true after she entered a contest, a beauty pageant, and won! McKenzie held out both arms and exclaimed, "This is the dress she wore when she was crowned!"

Winning that day changed the story of a little girl's life. She was able to travel the country, had so many adventures, and even received enough scholarships to go to college. Later, she became a nurse and helped many people for years to come.

"This magnificent woman is my grandmother, Margaret S. Fleming," said McKenzie pointing to her grandmother who was waiting in the wings. "Grandma taught me that ordinary people can do extraordinary things," McKenzie said with great pride. "You don't have to be famous to do something important. We all have the ability to accomplish great things. This is why I chose my grandmother as the person who most inspired me."

Everyone began clapping and yelling. McKenzie stepped away from the microphone and reenacted the crowning, waving to the audience. Her grandmother walked on stage and gave her a bouquet of snapdragons. The audience jumped to their feet and continued to give her a standing ovation.

As grandmother wiped tears of pride for McKenzie from her cheek, she recalled that special day years ago, when she first wore that same crown and how it changed her life forever.

McKenzie, gliding across the stage in her grandmother's dress that had been tucked away for so many years, was also remembering a special day - the day when she found a magical old trunk that inspired a little girl with its lifetime of memories.

Princess Notes

Princess Autographs

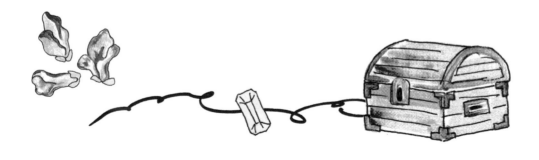

What the Experts are Saying about The Snapdragon Princess

The *Snapdragon Princess* is an uplifting story that will inspire children to discover the hero inside each of us!

-Ellen Langas Campbell, Author, *The Girls Know How®* series

I love this story because it reminds all of us that you don't have to read a history book to be inspired, your biggest inspiration could be sitting right next to you.

-Caitlin Friedman, Co-author of *HAPPY AT WORK, HAPPY AT HOME: The Girl's Guide to Being a Working Mom*

Kim is a great mother and role model to girls of all ages, and her children's tale is sweet and sentimental.
- Nancy Redd, *New York Times Bestselling Author of BODY DRAMA*

A heartwarming story of a young girl who finds inspiration and a role model in sometimes forgotten world for many... her family. Kudos in bringing the ones who are real role models to life.

-Carl Dunn, CEO, *Pageantry magazine/PromTime Magazine*

With *Snapdragon Princess*, Kim Parrish and Deb Landry capture that special connection between a girl and her grandmother, reaching across the generations to discover that they both share the dream of being a princess. And what girlfriend - whether she's 8 or 80 – hasn't wanted to glitter and shine? Every family has its own trunk with creaking hinges that contains a treasure trove of memories and history, and no politician or inventor or movie star's story could ever be more significant than that of a loved one. As the mother of two young girls, I love that this beautiful story is here to remind our daughters of this simple fact.

-Stacey S Schieffelin, Founder & President *ybf (your best friend), LLC*

Another beautifully written children's book from Deb Landry. *The Snapdragon Princess* is a heartwarming story of how real people can do anything their heart desires. An inspirational intergenerational tale that inspires young ladies to dream, create and cultivate a relationship that can never be broken.

- Elizabeth Hamilton-Guarino, *Mrs. Maine USA 06 CEO/Founder/Editor of www.BestEverYOU.com, Best Ever You Magazine*

I love reading stories that inspire us to keep dreaming big. This book shows us that ordinary people *can* do extraordinary things and we all are princesses in the hearts and minds of those who love us.

--Caitlin Brunell, *Miss America's Outstanding Teen 2008 and founder of Caitlin's Closet*

The *Snapdragon Princess* is a tale of genuine success. It combines imagination and history to demonstrate that no matter the circumstance, dreams really do come true. As the old saying goes, "To the world you may be one person, but to one person you may be the world." I endorse this book without reservation and shall recommend it to dreamers of all ages for many years to come.

-Tiffany E. Lawrence, *WV House of Delegates Member-58th District (Youngest woman ever to serve), Miss West Virginia 2006*

In a world where strong female role models aren't easy to find, Kim Parrish shows us that sometimes we need to look no further than our own backyards. *The Snapdragon Princess* is a delightful introduction to the idea of dreaming big, and reminds little girls (and grown-ups too) that no goal should ever be considered out of reach.

-Stacey Kole, Editor, *Savvy* Magazine

Featured in dozens of articles from *TV Guide* to *The New York Times*, Kim Parrish is a familiar face to millions who welcomed her into their homes throughout her eight years as a popular television host on QVC. During more than 6,000 hours of live TV appearances, she developed a rapport with viewers as well as celebrity guests and fashion trendsetters, and is recognized for her sense of style and sales savvy.

In 2005, she took aim at America's closets with the launch of the Kim Parrish Collection on HSN, her signature line of classic wardrobe basics noted for their innovative, updated twists. The collection is now featured on televised shopping channels in Canada and in Europe.

Touted as a "shopping goddess" by the media, Kim was Miss West Virginia 1992 and competed in the Miss America Pageant. In 2007, she became president of Miss America's Outstanding Teen organization, the "little sister" to the Miss America Pageant, and is working to develop it into the leading provider of scholarships for teenage girls in the nation. Kim is married to Craig Hartman and has a three-year old son, Chase. She's a dynamic public speaker, seasoned fashion writer and commentator and a passionate spokesperson. *The Snapdragon Princess* launches yet another genre of her talents. Learn more about Kim at www.brysontaylorpublishing.com, www.KimParrish.net or www.KimParrishCollection.com.

Deb Landry is the author of the best selling children's book, *Sticks Stones and Stumped, Yankee Go Home,* and the co-author of *The Comfort Zone* with Meline Kevorkian Ed.D., and Robin D'Antona, Ed.D. She is a freelance writer, blogger and parenting coach specializing in social awareness behaviors and character education and has authored several interactive children's mentoring plays on character education, social awareness, and bullying prevention.

A mother of four and grandmother of three, Deb spent 21 years in healthcare administration and 11 years as an after school director and founder of Crossroads. Although she is a certified parenting coach, she contributes her expertise to thirty-nine years of being a parent.

She passionately shares her expertise through lectures, workshops, books, author visits, blogging, and her parent coaching practice. With recognition and several awards for her work , Deb has been interviewed and featured on NBC, CBS, national radio, and several publications from USA Weekend Magazine, to Child Magazine.

Deb lives in New England with her husband Darrin and four children. For more information or to read her blogs visit, www.deblandry.com.

Christina St. Cyr was born and raised in New England. Inspired by the sights, sounds and colors of Coastal Maine where she lives with her husband and two daughters, Christina lends her artistic abilities to a variety of projects including graphic design, painting and culinary arts. Additionally, she is the Creative Services Manager for a network of websites and the founder/president of Pure Graphics Designs and Illustrations. Christina enjoys time with her family, balancing work with a passion for fitness, and time with friends. If you are ever on the coast of Maine, you may catch her kayaking or digging for clams along the beaches that inspire so much of her work. The Snapdragon Princess is Christina's second children's book.